GRuBtoWN taLes
Book Six

Splash, CRash aNd Loads of Cash

or

In Very Deep Water

A bit about the author

Philip Ardagh, whose very first **GRuBtoWN taLe** won him the Roald Dahl Funny Prize, is author of numerous books including the award-winning Eddie Dickens adventures, which have been translated into over 30 languages. He wrote BBC Radio's first truly interactive radio drama, collaborated with Sir Paul McCartney on his first children's book and is a 'regularly irregular' reviewer of children's books for the *Guardian*. Married with a son, he divides his time between Tunbridge Wells and Grubtown, where he cultivates his impressive beard.

Other children's books by Philip Ardagh published by Faber & Faber

GRuBtoWN taLes
Stinking Rich and Just Plain Stinky
The Year That It Rained Cows
The Far From Great Escape
The Wrong End of the Dog
Trick Eggs and Rubber Chickens

World Book Day Special Book
The Great Pasta Disaster

FICTION FOR 8+
The Eddie Dickens Trilogy
Awful End
Dreadful Acts
Terrible Times
The Further Adventures of Eddie Dickens
Dubious Deeds
Horrendous Habits
Final Curtain
Unlikely Exploits
The Fall of Fergal
Heir of Mystery
The Rise of the House of McNally

High In The Clouds
with Paul McCartney & Geoff Dunbar

NON-FICTION
The Hieroglyphs Handbook
Teach Yourself Ancient Egyptian
The Archaeologist's Handbook
The Insider's Guide To Digging Up The Past
Did Dinosaurs Snore?
100½ Questions about Dinosaurs Answered
Why Are Castles Castle-Shaped?
100½ Questions about Castles Answered

GRuBtoWN taLes
Book Six

Splash, CRash and
Loads of Cash

or

In Very Deep Water

by *Philip Ardagh*
Illustrated by Jim Paillot

ff

faber and faber

*Respectfully dedicated to the men and women of the
Royal National Lifeboat Institute who, fortunately for us,
are nothing like the coastguard at Limp!*

First published in 2010
by Faber and Faber Limited
Bloomsbury House
74-77 Great Russell Street
London
WC1B 3DA

Typeset by Faber and Faber Limited
Printed in England by Mackays of Chatham plc, Chatham, Kent

This is a work of fiction. Other than those clearly in the public
domain, all characters, businesses, places, properties, products,
organisations and even Grubtown itself are figments of the author's
imagination (with the possible exception of himself). Any similarities
to existing entities, past or present, are purely coincidental and
should not be inferred.

A CIP record for this book
is available from the British Library

ISBN 978–0–571–25349–4

2 4 6 8 10 9 7 5 3 1

A bit about Grubtown

You won't find Grubtown on any maps. The last time any mapmakers were sent anywhere near the place they were found a week later wearing nothing but pages from a telephone directory, and calling for their mothers. It's certainly a town and certainly grubby – except for the squeaky clean parts – but everything else we know about the place comes from Beardy Ardagh, town resident and author of these tales.

GRuBtoWN taLes were made possible
through the participation of the following
people, animals and organisations:

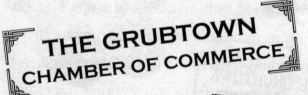

**THE GRUBTOWN
CHAMBER OF COMMERCE**

**THE GRUBTOWN
CHAMBER OF
HORRORS**

THE OFFICE
*of the Mayor
of Grubtown*

*THE SHED
of the Mayor
of Grubtown*

**OFFAL'S
SUNBEDS**

*The Mayor
of Grubtown
Himself*

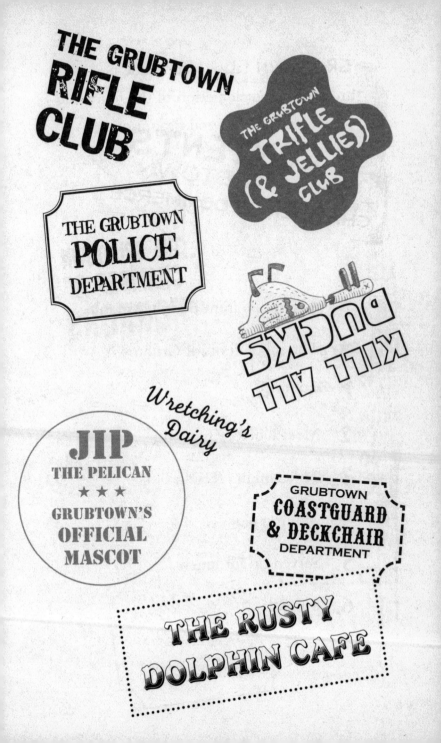

CONTENTS

★ A message from Beardy Ardagh 1

★ The inhabitants of Grubtown 3

1. All at sea 5

2. Meet Doctor Growbag 15

3. That sinking feeling 23

4. Making plans 33

5. Served up for lunch 45

6. Busted! 51

7. *Speeeed!* 63

8. Acting fast 71

9. Up, up and away! 85

10. Now what? 99

★ More words from Beardy Ardagh 113

★ (Just some of the folk) who pop up
in **GRuBtoWN taLes** 115

★ The delightful Beardy Ardagh tells of
other **GRuBtoWN taLes** 121

This page contains a missprint.

A message from
Beardy Ardagh

Just because there have been messages from me at the beginning of the other **GRuBtoWN taLes**, I've been told that there needs to be one here too. This is OUTRAGEOUS! I've far more important things to do, such as stuff cushions with my old beard hairs (to give as gifts) and take my troll for its injections. So, instead of my *blah, blah, blah-ing* on, here's the lyrics to one of the songs by Grubtown's very own Grumbly girls.

**'All Praise to Beardy Ardagh
(Who Don't Need to Work No Harder)
sung to the tune of
"We'll Gather Cucumbers Just As Soon
As I've Finished the Ironing'.**

1

No, I'm only joking. I wouldn't make you sit through that. I wouldn't make *Marley Gripe* sit through that and I like you a lot more than him.

In the third verse, the Grumbly girls actually try to make the word 'gold' rhyme with 'world' but make up for it in verse 322 by rhyming 'Flabby Gomez's meal' with 'glockenspiel' (which is a sort of xylophone).

I am relieved to report that the Grumbly girls don't appear in this particular **GRuBtoWN taLe**, which is good news for everyone involved. Their dad, Chumbly Grumbly, is in it though, but, if you want to find out more, you'll have to read on. (That's a hint for you to go now.)

Goodbye.

Beardy Ardagh.

Grubtown

The inhabitants
of Grubtown

At the back of the book (starting on page 115) you'll find a list of some of the people who live in Grubtown, including the Grumbly girls because – although they're not in this tale – they do live here. Okay?

Chapter One
All at Sea

Mayor Flabby Gomez realised they were sinking when the water came up to his ears.

'*Glublflublblblb!*' he said, which is what a gulp of surprise sounds like when spoken with a mouthful of seawater. And there was plenty of seawater to choose from. It was all around him. There was miles and miles and miles and millions of gallons of the stuff. A whole *sea* full, in fact.

It's said that when a person thinks he's

about to die, the whole of his life 'flashes in front of him' (or *her* if she's a she). If that's true, Flabby Gomez's flashback would have included plenty of eating and knitting. He *loves* eating and knitting.

The mayor wasn't the only one in trouble. There were four of them aboard the *Lazy Suzy* when it went down and, apart from young Mango Claptrap who had been sensible enough to climb to the very top of the mast, they were all in the water. The water was only up to Furl Claptrap's chin. He's Mango's dad and it was he who'd repaired the *Lazy Suzy*.

I use the term 'repaired' loosely (in the same way I might say 'cooked' when I really mean 'burnt'). Furl Claptrap is well-known throughout Grubtown for being able to do just about anything, but badly. He'd got the job of fixing up Lefty Scorn's boat because Luminous Shard, who usually fixes engines and patches up boats, had won a two-week trip to New Amsterdam for two people and a duck of his choice. He'd asked Furl Claptrap to look after the boatyard whilst he was away because, although Mango's dad is bad at repairing boats, at least he knows *how* to repair them. Well, that's how Shard tried to explain it later, when he was interviewed by the police.

The fourth person on board (but almost completely under water now) was Lefty Scorn himself. He runs the local laundrette and jewellery store over on Asphalt Street but liked to take the *Lazy Suzy* out at the weekend.

He certainly thought that he was going to drown.

I'm going to drown, he thought.

He wished that he'd bothered to wear a lifejacket. I expect they ALL wished that they'd been wearing lifejackets, except for Mango Claptrap. As well as being sensible enough to be at the top of the mast, he was also sensible enough to be wearing a lifejacket already, along with his usual pair of ridiculously short shorts.

Much to his own surprise, Flabby Gomez suddenly found himself floating. When the water came up to his eyes, he let go of the railing he'd been gripping with fear and bobbed up to the surface. Moments later, he was lying on his back staring up at the sky. Fortunately, all four of them had been up on the open deck when the *Lazy Suzy* – which was a small yacht, by the way – started taking in water, so none of them was trapped below deck.

Flabby Gomez floating on his back in the sea looked like a cross between one of those large fun inflatable thingumies you see hanging up outside beachfront stores and a small island. It was probably for that reason that Furl Claptrap and Lefty Scorn clambered on to him for safety. When the very tip of the yacht's mast finally disappeared beneath the surface – there were no real waves to speak of – Mango Claptrap bobbed on the surface next to them, holding on to the mayor's belt, so that he didn't drift away on the current.

Lefty Scorn had managed to send out a Mayday message over the radio before it went 'fizz' and stopped working altogether. A Mayday message is a general distress signal. In other words, what you're really saying is 'HELP! ANYONE WHO CAN HEAR THIS: HELP!!!!' but it sounds a lot more dignified and less panicky if you say, 'Mayday! Mayday!' so that's what Lefty Scorn had done. He'd followed this by giving the yacht's name and its rough location: 'This is the *Lazy Suzy*. We're about three hours out of Grubtown and I can see the funny rock shaped like a toaster to the west.'

Now all they had to do was wait. And hope. And not sink.

Lying staring up at the clear blue sky and feeling the water lapping around the edge of his body, Mayor Flabby Gomez felt strangely peaceful and proud. It was almost as though his large size and unusual buoyancy (as in floatability) had been leading up to this moment. His being a human island was saving lives!

Furl Claptrap found it quite pleasant sitting on the mayor, dangling his feet over the edge in the water. It was a nice warm sunny day and the sea was calm enough. This wasn't one of those sinkings because of bad weather, with waves crashing over the side of the yacht. This was sinking as a result of the yacht being put back together VERY BADLY. That was the one thing that was upsetting Mango's dad. He knew that the mess they were in was all his fault.

Lefty Scorn, who was sitting with his back to Furl Claptrap, his legs dangling over the other side of the floating mayor was feeling guilty for another reason. The *Lazy Suzy* was his yacht and the others were his guests ... the most important of whom was the mayor, on whom he was now *having to sit*. It was all very embarrassing.

'I'm sure we'll be rescued soon,' said Lefty Scorn. 'The coastguard over at Limp is bound to have heard our distress call.'

'I'm sure we shall,' said Flabby Gomez, sounding totally relaxed.

Bobbing in the water next to them, young Mango Claptrap suddenly became agitated and started waving his arms about. 'Shark!' he

shouted, pointing at a fin cutting through the
surface of the sea.

And he was right.

Chapter Two
Meet Doctor Growbag

Jilly Cheeter has been Mango Claptrap's best friend for as long as I can remember, so had she known that the *Lazy Suzy* had sunk with him on board, she'd have been really worried. As it was, she thought he was off having a great time and, the truth be told, may even have been a teeny-weenie bit jealous. But only a teeny-weenie bit, because they really, REALLY are such good friends.

While Mango was off sinking or drowning or being eaten by sharks, or whatever it was he was doing, Jilly was taking her dog Harvey to the vet. Harvey is a fairly large shaggy dog which means that, unless he has a lot of soapy baths, he spends a lot of time smelling of dog. Because he likes running around in the sea trying to bite waves, he also gets wet quite often. So he spends a lot of time smelling of *wet* dog.

The vet Jilly Cheeter was taking Harvey to see had only recently moved back to Grubtown to open his surgery. His name is Barty Growbag and he's very good with animals. He's also highly qualified, with lots of important letters after his name, such as MotPWLGiaWCC (Member of the People Who Look Good in a White Coat Club); PwP (Popular with Pets) and DMBBOiaW (Doesn't Mind Being Bitten Once in a While).

Jilly Cheeter was certainly impressed when she went into his surgery that very first time. The walls appeared to be covered with some very grand-looking framed certificates. It was only on later visits, when she had more of a chance to look at them, did she discover that not one of them has anything to do with being a vet. There was:

(i) A cycling proficiency certificate.

(ii) A boiler gas-safety certificate.

(iii) A giant money-off coupon for washing powder.

(iv) An 'I Survived The Giant Chomper Ride at Gnawing-Animals World' certificate.

(v) A cut-out 'I'm Truly Magical' certificate from

the back of a Whizzo
Junior Magician Set.

(vi) A rather nice square
of fancy wallpaper.

(vii) A pretend certi-
ficate that came with the
'frame-your-certificate-
here' frame.

But, boy, did they look good up on a wall!

'And why have you brought your dog –' he looked down at his notes to read the name '– Harvey to see me today?' asked Barty Growbag as he lifted Jilly Cheeter's dog onto the stainless-steel examination table.

'He won't eat,' explained Jilly, putting down her rucksack which had Harvey's favourite blanket and squeaky toy in it, 'and Harvey loves eating. That's probably his favourite pastime.'

Whilst Barty Growbag asked questions about Harvey, he gave the dog a thorough examination of everything from his teeth to his tummy to his waggy tail. He then returned to the tummy, gently feeling it with both hands. Harvey gave a little whimpering whine. 'Right,' he said. 'Then I think we'll have to give your dog an X-ray and, if he has got an obstruction, we'll have to have it removed.'

'Okay, Doctor Growbag,' she said.

Jilly Cheeter lives with her dad, Sloop Cheeter, and they don't have much money to pay, for example, expensive vet's bills. But they do have pet insurance. Mayor Flabby Gomez awarded it to Jilly one year for 'Services to Grubtown' (and it's much more useful than any medal).

Jilly Cheeter sat in the waiting room of the vet's surgery whilst a veterinary nurse took Harvey to be X-rayed. There were lots of old, dog-eared grown-ups' magazines on the table, full of boring subjects such as 'making your house look like a palace without spending a king's ransom' and 'adding a spark to your dinner party with gunpowder'. Jilly flipped through a few but when she came to a double-page spread about 'growing your own clothes' she decided to look at the posters instead.

The waiting room was covered with them. She was looking at one called 'Animals That Bite' when she heard a sort of 'squeak' and looked down. There, sitting on one of the waiting-room chairs and nibbling the corner of a magazine about hamster wheels, was a larger-than-average, rat. He – and she knew he was a he – was looking back up at her with a look in its eyes far more intelligent than the look most people in Grubtown give you (naming no names).

'Hi, Free-Kick,' said Jilly Cheeter.

The rat appeared to raise a paw in greeting.

Maybe not.

Chapter Three
That sinking feeling

The second time Mango Claptrap shouted 'Shark!' it was his turn to get a mouthful of seawater. He'd read somewhere that drinking seawater can drive you mad but he reckoned that he wouldn't have time to drink enough to find out. He would be eaten by the shark long before then.

Moments later, he felt himself being yanked up on to Flabby Gomez by his father, Furl. It was a bit of a tight squeeze on the floating mayor with three of them up there but there was no time to complain.

'Now row for your lives!' shouted Furl Claptrap.

He thrust a makeshift oar into his son's hand. Mango noticed that it was the sign for the *Lazy Suzy*, a long thin piece of wood which should have been screwed to the side of the boat. It turns out that his dad had not only used glue to fix it in place instead, but a cheap glue which dissolved in water . . . which was lucky for them, because it had bobbed to the surface and made a good oar. Lefty Scorn was using the mop which was used to 'swab the decks'. Furl was using a huge wooden paddle which was for sliding pizzas in and out of the special pizza clay oven at **UPSTAIRS AT AMPLE SAKI'S**. How it had ended up floating along in the middle of the sea is a mystery. **UPSTAIRS AT AMPLE SAKI'S** isn't even a beachside restaurant. AND it's upstairs.

Furl, Lefty and Mango found that they were rowing the mayor around in circles until Mango barked a few commands and got them all rowing together in the same direction at (roughly) the same time.

'One, two, three, *row*! One, two, three, *row*! One, two, three, *row*!' he shouted.

Mayor Flabby Gomez, meanwhile, rather liked the fact that he was now gliding through the water at quite an impressive speed without having to do any of the work. Now that Mango was aboard him, though, Flabby was a little lower in the water and then, of course, there was the rather serious – rather sharp-toothed – matter of the shark.

'Maybe it's someone having a laugh!' said Furl Claptrap, still frantically rowing.

'Having a laugh?' asked Lefty Scorn.

'You know,' said Furl. 'A swimmer with a joke shark's fin strapped to his back.'

'In the middle of the ocean?' said Lefty Scorn in disbelief. He wanted to call Furl Claptrap an 'idiot' but just managed to stop himself in time. Rowing on a floating mayor whilst being chased by a shark wasn't the best time or place to be starting an argument.

As if to prove that it wasn't a swimmer with a joke shark's fin strapped to its back, the shark chose that moment to stick its nose above the water.

Mango, who was looking over his shoulder as he frantically paddled with the *Lazy Suzy* sign, caught a glimpse of it. The shark grinned at him. It didn't seem to be a particularly friendly grin, and it showed off the creature's impressive rows of teeth.

'O-One, two, three, *row*! One, two, three, *row*!' shouted Mango, wanting to keep them in rhythm ... wanting to keep them *moving*.

'We could throw it some bait,' said Flabby Gomez, which gave Mango Claptrap a bit of a surprise. He'd been so busy concentrating on the rowing that he'd almost forgotten that the thing they were rowing was a human being, even if it was a very large and very floaty one.

'What could we use as bait, Mr Mayor?' asked Mango. 'One, two, three, *row*! One, two, three, *row*!'

'I have a range of delicious snacks in my money belt,' said Flabby Gomez.

'The kind of snacks a hungry shark might like?' asked Mango Claptrap. 'One, two, three, *row*! One, two, three, *row*!'

'Absolutely!' said the mayor, his mind distracted from the danger for a moment at the thought of food. 'Including Jip and Binkey's favourite, smoked mackerel pâté.' Jip and Binkey are pelicans, Jip being Grubtown's official mascot and Binkey his mate.

'Are you still wearing the belt around your waist?' asked Mango Claptrap. 'One, two, three, *row*! One, two, three, *row*!'

'Yes,' said the Mayor, 'though I can't take it off with you three sitting on me like this.'

'But maybe *I* can,' said Mango. 'Dad, you and Mr Scorn must keep rowing.'

'Okay—' said his dad, but he sounded uncertain.

'Go for it!' said Lefty Scorn, both hands still clutching his mop oar.

So Mango Claptrap, in bright orange life-jacket and ridiculously short shorts, squeezed his way between the two rowers on Flabby Gomez's tummy and finally managed to unbuckle the mayor's money belt.

'One, two, three, *row*! One two, three, *row*!'

He tried to pull it free but it was caught on something.

'One, two, three, *row*! One two, three, *row*!'

Mango gave the belt another YANK!

This time, it not only came free but also went flying out of Mango Claptrap's hand into the water.

'One, two, th—'

Furl Claptrap and Lefty Scorn stopped rowing and watched.

The shark didn't even give the money belt a second glance as it sank beneath the waves ...

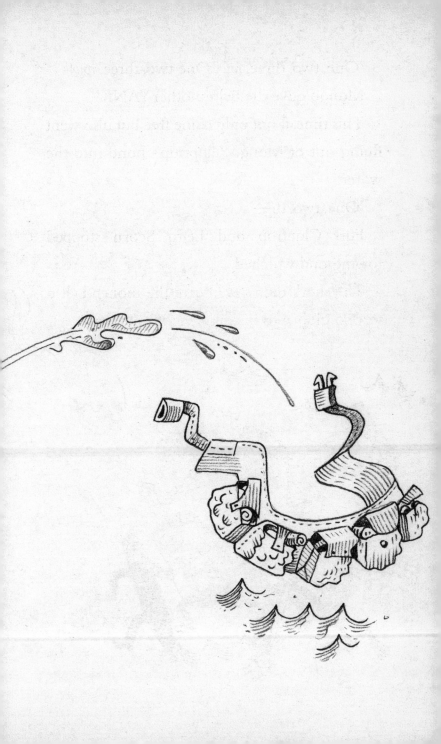

Chapter Four
Making plans

In Grubtown, there is a group of escaped lab rats living in a shed over on Disappointment Avenue. When I first started writing these **GRuBtoWN taLes**, they lived on the top floor of an eight-storey garden shed, with Mayor Flabby Gomez and his family – wife Pritt and son Tundra – living on the bottom six floors (with the seventh used for storage). The Gomezes were living there while Flabby was knitting them a new home. Now that house has been completed and the mayor and family have moved into it, the Grubtown rats have the whole shed to themselves.

As well as being a little larger and quite a bit shaggier than your average rat, they're also a lot brainier. Their leader is called Free-Kick and his mate is called Lulu. The rats were given their names by Emily Blotch, the girl who helped them to escape.

You often see them around town, though never rummaging through litter nor getting under your feet. They're about as friendly and polite as any rats can be, as Free-Kick proved whilst sitting quietly in the waiting room of Dr Barty Growbag's surgery, waiting for his annual check-up (while Dr Growbag was seeing to Harvey).

Just about the only person in Grubtown who *isn't* proud of our rats is Wide Brim Petty-Mandrake (Grubtown's undertaker and chief whinger). He actually wrote to the laboratory over in Werty to tell them where their escaped rats were hiding out. Not only that, he also told them who had helped them escape. It was this last part which led to his letters never reaching the laboratory. (Not that he knew that.) I think there's some important explaining to be done. And I'm just the (bearded) man to do it:

Condo Blotch used to be a cleaner. Cleaners don't get paid much money. (I should know, I used to be one too.) Because Condo is a single mum, with Emily to look after, she had to do more than one cleaning job to make enough to feed and clothe them both and have a roof over their heads. Every evening (six days a week), Condo and Emily took the bus over to the nearby village of Werty and then walked the last bit of the way to the **Doohickey & Squat** laboratories.

(Condo couldn't afford a babysitter for Emily.) Every evening, Paul the security guard would let them in and Emily would be made to wait in reception with Paul while her mum went and cleaned. And every evening, Paul would sit with Emily for about fifteen minutes before having to go off on his rounds to check everything was safe and sound, and every evening Emily would be back in reception in time for him and her mother to find her there.

What Condo Blotch didn't know and Paul the security guard didn't know was that, after exploring the whole building during the first few nights – being careful to keep out of sight from her mother – Emily Blotch visited the same room every time. It was the room behind the door marked:

**STRICTLY NO ADMITTANCE
AUTHORISED PERSONNEL
ONLY**

On the wall next to the door was one of those keypads where you have to punch in an entry code for the door to unlock.

The first time she saw it, Emily punched in the numbers of her birthday. When that didn't work – and there was no way she'd expected it to – she tried typing in: 1-2-3-4-5.

There was a loud 'CLICK', which she didn't hear, and, to her utter amazement, the door unlocked.

Inside, she found the rats in their cages.

Miss Emily Blotch fell in love with those rats the first time she laid eyes on them and, I suspect, they felt the same way about her. She chatted away happily to them, using both speech and the sign language that she and her mum use to talk to each other. (Emily is profoundly deaf.)

I don't know when exactly she hatched the plan to help Free-Kick and the others escape, but it wasn't long before she was training them for that day. Every evening, she'd get them out of their cages and practise how they were going to do it. She'd have them lining up, jumping, crouching and wriggling on her instructions. Within a month or so, they were a well-rehearsed team.

Next, little Emily Blotch had to convince her mother, Condo, to let her bring her favourite toy – a great big dolls' house that Condo had built her in what little spare time she had – to the labs. She took a bit of persuading.

Of course, Emily had no intention of playing with the dolls' house at the lab. Every evening, Paul would get it out of his cupboard for her and put it on the floor in reception and every evening she would say 'Thank you!' and wait for him to go off on his rounds. Then she would carry the dolls' house to the room with the door marked:

STRICTLY NO ADMITTANCE
AUTHORISED PERSONNEL
ONLY

and punch in the entry code: 1-2-3-4-5.

Often, Emily would find Free-Kick and Lulu and a few of the other braver rats already out of their cages sitting on the workbench eagerly waiting for her. She was teaching them how to lean through the bars and open the clasp locks on their cages, and some learnt quicker than others. That way, when the day came – and she had no idea when the day would be, of course – she could give the instruction, and they'd all let themselves out of their cages and be ready to run!

Once they were all out of their cages, she had them practise fitting inside the dolls' house together. It was a tight squeeze and took weeks and weeks of practice to get it right. With one rat in the wrong place or too much pushing and shoving, a tell-tale rat's tail might stick through one of the little windows or, worse still, cause the whole hinged front of the house to swing open and give away their hiding place.

Finally, they got it perfect. With all the rats out of the cages, little Emily Blotch would give the signal and they'd all hurry inside the dolls' house in strict order and take up their pre-arranged positions. Emily would then swing the front wall of the dolls' house shut and flip the little brass hook through the little brass eye

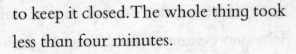

to keep it closed. The whole thing took less than four minutes.

But there was a problem.

The dolls' house was far too heavy for Emily to carry on her own once the rats were in it. Now that she'd trained them how to fit inside the house, she started the far riskier part of the plan: training them to run from their room to the reception, where they could *then* hide in the dolls' house.

It didn't take long for them to learn the route – the rats had to find their way around mazes as part of the experiments in the labs – but on a number of occasions they almost ran into Emily's mum, Condo, or Paul doing his rounds.

Then, one day, Emily Blotch decided that they were ready. She would just have to wait for the right opportunity . . .

. . . which finally came when, on entering the labs one evening, Paul offered to give them a lift home afterwards.

'I've been here all day for a meeting about new security measures,' he said, 'and I'm going to stay with my brother Hepcat in Grubtown tonight. I'm happy to drive you home. It'll be no trouble.'

Emily couldn't believe her luck!

'We could take my dolls' house home,' she said, innocently. 'It would save us having to take it on the bus and I'm bored of playing with it *every* night.'

With her mum off cleaning and Paul off on his rounds, Emily swung open the front of the dolls' house on the floor in reception, positioning it just where the rats had rehearsed, and dashed to the door marked:

STRICTLY NO ADMITTANCE
AUTHORISED PERSONNEL
ONLY

She punched in: 1-2-3-4-5.

Nothing happened.

The entry code had been changed.

'Now what?' said Flabby Gomez who, like the other three survivors of the sunken yacht, was looking at the bubbles on the surface of the sea where his food-packed money belt had just sunk.

'One, two, three, *row*! One, two, three, *row*!'

'I'd have expected smoked mackerel pâté sandwiches to float,' said Furl Claptrap. 'Not your fault, son.'

'One, two, three, *row*! One, two, three, *row*!'

But Mango Claptrap couldn't help feeling guilty. He'd been the one who'd let the belt slip through his fingers after yanking it free from around the mayor's waist.

'No, not YOUR fault, Mango,' said Lefty Scorn. Although he only spoke the five words 'No, not YOUR fault, Mango', everyone on board Flabby Gomez – and Flabby Gomez himself – also distinctly heard the eleven unspoken words: 'but YOURS, Furl, for fixing up the *Lazy Suzy* so badly.'

'One, two, three, *row*! One, two, three, *row*!'

'Does anyone else have any food on them?' began the mayor. Then he stopped. 'Look!' he said. 'The shark's stopped following us. It's turning away.'

The mayor was right. The shark had swerved away from them and now completely disappeared under the water. Flabby Gomez imagined a shark's eye view of what was going on below the surface. It would be looking up at the nearest object: HIM, the underside of a large floating mayor.

'Where *is* that creature?' he shouted.

'Quiet, everyone!' said Mango, who'd been trying to remember everything he'd ever learnt about sharks. 'Sharks are attracted by noise and movement. Let's stop rowing and be – *Ssshhhhh*!'

His father lifted the pizza paddle clear of the water, as did Lefty Scorn and his deck-mop, and Mango and the *Lazy Suzy* sign. Their floating island – also known as Mayor Flabby Gomez – drifted silently forward.

They waited.

Nervously.

Wondering where the shark was and what it would do nex–

The sea to Flabby's left erupted and the shark broke through the surface, thrashing its body

and twisting its tail. It had the money belt in its mouth and was ripping open the black canvas with its teeth as if it was nothing more than tissue paper. Sandwiches, cakes and chocolate bars spilled everywhere.

The shark fell back down into the sea, mouth

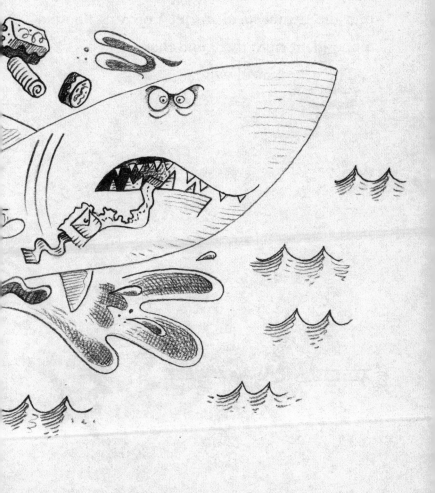

wide open, swallowing down the mayor's snacks and surrounding seawater in one mighty gulp.

All four Grubtowners were thinking the same: that this wouldn't be enough to satisfy a great big shark's appetite. To a shark like that, it'd be like a handful of peanuts before the actual meal, and the actual meal in question was floating alongside it right there and then.

The actual meal was *them*.

Chapter Six
Busted!

Emily Blotch tried punching in the numbers on the keypad a second time: 1-2-3-4-5, and then again and again. The door didn't budge. What was it Paul the security guard had said? He'd been there all day for a meeting about 'new security measures'. And one of these new security measures must have been to change the entry code at the door marked:

**STRICTLY NO ADMITTANCE
AUTHORISED PERSONNEL
ONLY**

Changed to something a little less obvious than 1-2-3-4-5.

Emily wanted to scream.

She couldn't believe her bad luck. Of all the days they chose to change the code, it was the day that was perfect opportunity for her beloved rats to escape from **Doohickey & Squat**.

She tried entering her birthday date again.

No.

Then she tried 5-4-3-2-1.

No.

0-2-4-6-8.

No.

0-1-3-7-9.

No.

Then she started punching in random numbers in random orders.

No.

No.

No.

No.

'NO!!!'

The door wouldn't budge.

But she didn't give in. She kept on trying and trying.

Then, quite unexpectedly, there was a loud 'CLICK', which she didn't hear . . .

. . . and the door swung open.

But how was that possible? Emily hadn't even just punched in another random set of numbers . . .

Then she saw her answer. The door had been opened from the *inside*, which didn't require a code, just someone to turn the handle.

There in front of her was a pyramid of rats, reaching up to handle-height with Free-Kick and Lulu at the very top.

And did Free-Kick sign the word 'Hello' with his tiny paws when he saw Emily framed in the doorway?

She can't be 100 per cent sure.

But she likes to think so.

And so do I. And I'm the one telling this tale.

'We've got to hurry,' said Emily, proud beyond proud that all the rats had either been able to get out of their own cages or been helped by the others . . . and had OPENED THE LAB DOOR.

They darted down darkened corridors, dashed across open hallways, keeping to the shadows as much as possible, until they finally reached the dolls' house and, just as they'd practised hundreds of times before, they dashed inside it.

Emily swung the front shut and flipped the brass hook into the brass eye.

Phase One of the rescue mission was complete.

When Paul came back from his security

rounds and her mum had finished that night's cleaning, Emily was already waiting by the double doors with the dolls' house at her feet.

'All set to go, I see,' asked Paul, making sure he spoke the words in front of the little girl so that she could read his lips.

'Yes,' she nodded.

'Humdrum should be here any minute,' said Paul. Humdrum Topaz was the security guard who was taking over for the rest of the night shift.

She arrived on her motorbike a few minutes later and it was time for them to go. Paul lifted the dolls' house.

'Phew! This is heavy,' he said. 'What have you got in here, Emily? Rock cakes?'

Emily smiled and signed the word 'toys', which her mum translated for the security guard.

They walked across the car park. It turned out that Paul had a van, not a car.

Emily wanted to be alone, so she volunteered to sit in the back, while her mum, Condo, sat in the passenger seat up front next to Paul.

'I'll get you a rug,' Paul told Emily. 'It's getting a bit chilly.'

The moment he disappeared down the side of the van, Emily Blotch flipped open the brass hook which had been holding the front of the dolls' house closed.

'Go,' she whispered to the rats packed as tight as sardines. 'You're free.' She pointed to the open back doors of the van.

Not one rat moved, except for Free-Kick. And all free-Kick did was shake his head.

They weren't going anywhere.

They were staying with their Emily.

By the time the security guard had got back with the rug, the little girl was hugging her dolls' house with a MASSIVE smile on her face.

Grubtown isn't full of the brightest folk in the world but it didn't take us long to realise that the rats that had escaped from the lab over in Werty – mentioned in all the papers, including our two local ones* – and the rats that had moved into Flabby's shed must be one and the same. (Especially because Emily came to visit them often.) But Flabby Gomez took an

*The Grubtown Daily Herald and
The Grubtown Weekly Gerald

instant liking to the rats. And Flabby Gomez is not only Mayor of Grubtown but he also owns it. And Flabby Gomez instructed Chief of Police Grabby Hanson that each and every one of those rodents had been made an honorary citizen of Grubtown and should be 'afforded all the rights and protections that go with being a citizen'. In other words, if the rats wanted to stay, no one but Flabby Gomez himself could have them removed.

When outsiders came asking if anyone had seen any escaped rats, and later came saying that they'd had reports about some extra large, extra shaggy rats living in Grubtown, Grubtowners everywhere looked them square in the eyes and said, 'What rats?'

Even the members the Fox family who HATE just about everyone in Grubtown kept their mouths shut. The reason? Because, as owners of a specialist store called KILL ALL DUCKS, they hate ducks more than anyone and anything in the world. And Derek Fox, the father, had read somewhere that rats often steal ducks' eggs. The thought of this made the Foxes – and still makes the Foxes – very happy indeed.

The only Grubtowner who thought the rats should be back behind bars was Wide Brim Petty-Mandrake (Grubtown's undertaker and chief whinger). He was forever writing to the local press* about the sea not being blue enough, or park keepers not being tall enough, or council notices being printed on paper that 'smells funny'. Then, one day, he decided to write to the **Doohickey & Squat** laboratories to not only tell them where their rats were, but who had helped them escape and how. The story was now common knowledge around town.

What isn't common knowledge is that Grubtown's postman reads each of Wide Brim Petty-Mandrake's letters before deciding

*The Grubtown Daily Herald and
The Grubtown Weekly Gerald

whether to deliver it or not. He puts them into two piles: **DELIVER** and **BURN**.

The reason for this is straightforward enough. Wide Brim Petty-Mandrake posts HUNDREDS of letters a week. Most of them are complaining to people about this, that and the other, and the postman KNOWS full-well that they'll go straight in the bin once they've been opened anyway. He's not as young as he used to be, and the last thing he wants to be doing is lugging around a heavy sack – which is bad for his back – when what's

weighing him down is a bunch of letters from Wide Brim Petty-Mandrake which no one will want to read anyway.

When the postman read the letter to **Doohickey & Squat** and saw that IT NAMED EMILY BLOTCH AS THE CULPRIT, it went straight in the **BURN** pile.

You see, our postman's name is Hepcat Lutz and his brother Paul is a very good friend of Condo and Emily Blotch. Back then Paul was a security guard over at the labs.

It's a small world, ain't it?

Chapter Seven
Speeeed!

Police Chief Grabby Hanson was lying on his side on the floor, propped up on an elbow, gazing at the treasure trove of stolen silver teapots under the bed when he got the phone call about the *Lazy Suzy* being in trouble.

The call came from the coastguard over in Limp.

'But why are you telling me?' asked Grabby Hanson. 'There's nothing I can do. You're the guys with the lifeboat and the helicopter.'

'Because your mayor was on board the yacht when they sent out their Mayday message.'

Chief Hanson let the duvet cover flap back over the side of the bed and got to his feet. 'Mayor Gomez is on board a sinking yacht?'

'He could be in the sea by now,' said the Limp coastguard. 'It sounds like the *Lazy Suzy* was sinking fast.'

'I'm on my way,' said Hanson. He took one last look at his handsome features reflected in

a particularly fine Georgian silver teapot, lying on his duvet, before picking it up and putting it under his bed with the rest of them.

He'd stolen them all earlier that day from the Grubtown Museum where they were holding an exhibition called VERY RARE AND STEALABLE TEAPOTS FROM ALL OVER THE PLACE, and taken them home in the back of his Chief of Police car (hidden under some anti-crime posters). He'd been just about to hand himself in and ask himself a few questions down at the police station, under caution, when the phone had rung.

Slipping his mobile phone back into his pocket, he unclipped the police walkie-talkie from his belt and headed out towards his car parked in the driveway. 'Chief Hanson to Constable Gelatine. Are you receiving me? Over.'

'Chief? This is Officer Tripwire, receiving you loud and clear.'

'Where's Constable Gelatine?' said Grabby

Hanson, climbing into his vehicle. 'I want Gelatine.'

Mustard Tripwire was silent for a moment before answering. *'Uncle's got a bit of a tummy upset. He's – er – in the –'*

'Never mind, Tripwire. You'll have to do,' said the Chief. 'First off, tell Gelatine that I have a lead on the teapot thefts and expect to make an arrest soon.' He put the key in the ignition and fired up the engine.

'That's great news, Chief. Are you the thief?'

'Good police work, Mustard! I most certainly *am* my number-one suspect, but there are a few loose ends which need tying up.' Grabby Hanson fumbled his walkie-talkie and narrowly avoided running down a duck. It's illegal to drive around Grubtown talking into a mobile phone, unless it's hands-free, but Grabby had made sure that there was nothing in the laws about police radios.

'Is there anything else, Chief?'

'There most definitely is. Mayor Gomez, Lefty Scorn, Mango and Furl Claptrap need rescuing out at sea. Meet me aboard the *Bovine Beauty* at Rotten Quay. If you get there before me, get her fuelled and ready to go.'

'*Sure, Chief,*' said Officer Tripwire.

The *Bovine Beauty* is a police launch – a fast police boat – which used to belong to Clam Wretching, founder of Wretching's Dairy. This may explain why it's painted white with black blotches to look like a cow. (By the way, seafaring folk usually calls ships, boats and floating things – except mayors – 'she'. Don't ask me why.)

'*Okay, Chief,*' *said Tripwire.* '*I'll have her ready . . . but why do we need to go out there? Surely the coastguard will reach them long before we do?*'

'Because he's our mayor, Tripwire, and we love him . . . and he pays our wages.'

'*I'm on it, Chief.*'

'Good lad,' said Grabby Hanson. He was

behind an open-backed truck piled high with duck feed. He gave a quick blast of siren so that it would pull over and let him past.

Less than fifteen minutes later, Police Chief Grabby Hanson was jumping down from a wooden jetty into the police launch next to Officer Mustard Tripwire, and they were off.

Less than half an hour after that, Tripwire raised his arm and pointed to a dot in the sky. 'Look, Chief!' he said. 'Isn't that the coastguard helicopter?'

'No,' said the police chief, 'I think you'll find it's a bird. But I admire your enthusiasm.'

Sure enough, Jip the pelican flew more clearly into view.

'He's got something in his mouth, Chief,' said Tripwire. 'And I don't think it's a fish.'

Grabby Hanson steered the *Bovine Beauty* with one hand and with the other held up the pair of binoculars he had hanging around his neck. He cut the engine and brought the speed boat to a halt. 'Here, Jip! Jip! Jip! Jip! Jip!' he called.

Jip came swooping straight down at the sound of his name. He landed on the chrome trim of the speedboat's tiny windscreen and opened his beak. Something big and floppy fell at Grabby Hanson's feet.

Officer Tripwire bent down, picked it up and handed it to the chief. It was a cap with the word '**COASTGUARD**' woven above the peak. A peak with a bite out of it. Inside the cap, written in pen in wobbly letters was one word: **SHARK**.

'Oh dear,' said Mustard Tripwire. 'What do you think it means?'

'Take a wild guess,' said Grabby Hanson, as the engine roared back to life and he headed the speedboat further out to sea.

Chapter Eight
Acting fast

Jilly Cheeter was with Doctor Barty Growbag when she first heard about the *Lazy Suzy* being in trouble. Barty Growbag was showing Jilly the X-ray of Harvey's tummy.

'See that outline which looks like a size-eleven slipper?' he asked, holding the X-ray up to the light of the window.

'Yes,' said Jilly Cheeter.

'That's a size-eleven slipper,' said the vet. 'And this thing,' he said, pointing to a grey garden-sprinkler-shaped area on the X-ray, 'is a garden sprinkler.'

HARVEY

'Is that a medal?' asked Jilly, pointing at the bottom of the X-ray.

'I believe it is,' said the vet.

'I was wondering where that one got to,' said Jilly.

'Well, it ended up inside your dog, Harvey, along with all this other gubbins,' said Barty Growbag. 'No wonder he's unwell. He'll need an operation, and then he'll be as right as rain.'

The reception desk in the waiting room was being staffed by one of Purple and Hind-Leg Outing's many children. (They've lost count how many they have, but they love them all and – being so incredibly rich – none of them has to work if they don't want to.) Sandy Outing loves animals and works part-time at Barty Growbag's surgery for nothing. She was busy sorting out a new filing system and had the radio on in the background. There was a newsflash about the mayor.

'Blimey!' she said.

'What is it, Sandy?' asked the vet, because he knew that Miss Outing wasn't someone who said 'Blimey!' rather loudly unless it was something serious.

'It's the mayor!' said Sandy Outing. 'He's on Lefty Scorn's yacht and they've sent out a Mayday message. Apparently, it's sinking. The coastguard are on their way and everything.'

'Mango!' said Jilly Cheeter, snatching her

rucksack off a chair and putting it on her back. 'Will you look after Harvey, please, Mr Growbag?' she asked. 'And give him that operation as soon as possible?'

'Certainly, Jilly, but where are you going – ?' But the vet was talking to thin air. Jilly Cheeter was already halfway out of the door.

She ran around the corner to the offices of Grubtown Cars. There was a battered old taxi with its 'FOR HIRE' light on parked outside and she jumped right in.

'Can you take me to the airport as quickly as possible, please?' asked Jilly Cheeter. 'It's urgent. I don't have any money on me at the moment, but my dog's swallowed a medal which you can have once the vet's got it out of his tummy.'

'Tempting though you make that sound, Jilly, I'll take you to the airport for nothing,' said the driver, turning around to face her with a friendly grin.

'Oh, hello, Mr Grumbly,' said Jilly. 'Thank you

very much.' The driver was Chumbly Grumbly, father of the Grumbly girls who are famous throughout Grubtown for writing terrible songs and singing them just as badly.

He pulled out into the traffic with a screech of tyres and sped off down the road. 'Your dad's not in any trouble, is he?' he asked, glancing back at her in his rear-view mirror. (She could see a reflection of his impressively bushy eyebrows.)

'Hasn't he got a job at the airport?'

'No, it's not Dad,' said Jilly Cheeter and she went on to explain everything above the noise of the engine, and all the strange rattles and bumps the battered old taxi made when moving at high speed.

Don't get any grand ideas about Grubtown Airport or, to give the place its correct title, FLABBY GOMEZ INTERNATIONAL AIRPORT or FLAB-GO INTERNATIONAL. We're very proud of it, of course. It had only been open a few months when this tale took place, not that it's changed that much since then. Maybe they've added some more giant photographs of Flabby Gomez's smiling face and some fake grass and plastic trees, but it's still pretty much a runway, a control tower, an aircraft hangar and a few shed-like buildings used as arrival and departure lounges with a gift shop. (Lounges in this case mean cramped spaces with a few plastic chairs.)

The airport was originally a private landing strip for Flabby Gomez's father, Big Man Gomez, who used to smuggle stuff in by plane at the dead of night. When he died, the place was pretty much forgotten. Flabby Gomez finds it hard enough to fit inside an aeroplane, let alone want to fly in one. Then one day Purple Outing (multi-millionaire owner of **PURPLE OUTING'S MUSIC SHACK**) thought it might be fun to open it up again so that he could fly all over the place to buy old vinyl records and to go and see bands.

In the end – with a lot of money from Purple Outing – Mayor Flabby Gomez re-opened the airstrip as Grubtown's public airport and now anyone can use it, so long as they want to fly to or from the handful of places on its routes. Most of the flights are cheap enough, but the airport tax (which goes straight to Flabby Gomez) is quite expensive. And so are the gifts in the FLAB-GO INTERNATIONAL gift shop.

For the price of an **I'VE FLOWN FROM FLAB-GO INTERNATIONAL AND SURVIVED**' T-shirt you could probably buy three decent T-shirts from Margo's multi-purpose store.

When they arrived at the airport, Chumbly Grumbly drove all the way up to the control tower, ignoring all the 'NO ENTRY', 'CAUTION: DUCKS CROSSING', 'KEEP OUT', 'FLABBY GOMEZ FOR MAYOR' and 'AIRPORT STAFF ONLY'-type signs along the way. He screeched to a halt with a cloud of burning tyre rubber and exhaust fumes, and they lurched forwards in their seats.

'Thanks, Mr Grumbly!' said Jilly Cheeter. 'That was fast!' She was already half out of the car, and was now running up to the entrance to the control tower.

Jilly found her dad, Sloop Cheeter, playing a game of cards with a man wearing a very impressive aircraft captain's uniform. When Jilly looked more closely at the captain's cap badge, she could see that it was made of the gold-foil wrapping from a chocolate coin.

'Oh, hello, Jilly,' said Sloop Cheeter, looking up mildly surprised. 'Is Harvey okay?'

'He's fine, Dad, said Jilly. 'Well, he's swallowed a size-eleven slipper, a garden sprinkler and one of my medals, but Doctor Growbag says he'll be fine once they've been taken out.'

'Then why *are* you here?' asked Sloop Cheeter, which was an ideal opportunity for Jilly to explain everything.

'And you think I can just lend you a pilot and a plane to go searching for Mango and the others?' asked her dad when she'd finished.

'Well, we can't do NOTHING!' said Jilly.

'Captain Preen is the only one here who knows how to fly a plane and the reason he's sitting up here with me is because his is being fixed. A wing fell off again. I've got a departure lounge full of angry passengers. There are no other planes.'

Just then, with a twitch of his whiskers, Free-Kick climbed out of Jilly's rucksack. Before she even had a chance to say, 'Hi, Free-Kick!' or 'How did you get in there?' the rat had jumped up on to the windowsill that went all the way around the tower.

An airport control tower is a bit like a lighthouse. The top is one big room with huge glass windows all the way around so that the controllers can look out and see what's happening down on the runway and up in the sky. Free-Kick started running clockwise around the sill, stopping occasionally and staring through the glass as though he was looking for something. Finally, he stopped and stood up on his hind legs, rubbing the window with his front paws.

Jill dashed over to him and looked out.

She gasped. 'But what about that, Dad?' she asked. She pointed through the glass.

The 'that' she was pointing at was a huge helium-filled balloon with a basket underneath it big enough to carry about six people. It was tied to big metal pegs hammered into the ground on a patch of lawn by the runway.

The balloon itself was white with the very familiar **STOP BEING QUITE SO FAT** logo painted right across it in big, big letters.

Now, just in case you're one of the few people on this planet who don't already know it, the **STOP BEING QUITE SO FAT** business empire is made up of the **STOP BEING QUITE SO FAT** soft drinks range (drunk in over one hundred countries around the world) and the **STOP BEING QUITE SO FAT** keep-fit centres, which can be found in seventy-five capital cities, and plenty of other places besides. This helium-filled balloon – which is like a hot-air balloon but doesn't need a burner to keep it afloat – belongs to the founder, owner and Chief Executive Officer of **STOP BEING**

QUITE SO FAT, a certain Condo Blotch who is now very, very rich. Yes, the selfsame Condo Blotch who used to clean, amongst other places, the **Doohickey & Squat** labs over in Werty, former home of the Grubtown rats. Ms Blotch and her daughter Emily live in many beautiful houses all over the world – you've probably seen photos of them in glossy magazines (next to adverts for perfumes with very silly names) – but the house in Grubtown is the one they call home.

And Condo Blotch must have been in town because here was her balloon sitting to the side of the runway at Grubtown's airport. Condo and Emily love ballooning.

'You want me to ask Condo to fly you out to sea in her *balloon*?' Sloop Cheeter asked his daughter.

'Why not, Dad?' said Jilly. 'The *Lazy Suzy* sent out a Mayday message. If Condo Blotch was on a ship in the area, she'd have headed straight for them . . . so why not ask to use her balloon?'

'But –'

'But what, Dad?' Jilly Cheeter interrupted her father. 'You've known Condo most of your life. You went to school with her, back in the days when we *had* schools in Grubtown.'

'She has a point, Sloop,' said Captain Teakwood Preen. 'There's no harm in asking.'

So that's exactly what Sloop Cheeter did.

Chapter Nine
Up, up and away!

After Sloop Cheeter had managed to contact Condo Blotch and get her permission – which she was very willing to give – he would only let Jilly go in the balloon if Captain Teakwood Preen went with her.

The captain seemed even more excited than she was. 'I've always wanted to fly one of these!' he said.

Jilly eyed the pretend badge on his cap. 'You really are a pilot, aren't you, Captain Preen?' she asked.

'You'd better believe it!' he said. 'But

I've no idea how to fly a helium balloon!'

It was while they were walking around the large wicker basket that Jilly Cheeter spotted an old fishing boat just inside the entrance of the aircraft hangar. A half-formed plan immediately sprang into her mind. What if they could swap the basket for the old boat and, if they found Mango and the others, *land it in the sea*?

When her dad had got Condo Blotch's permission, she hadn't said anything about letting them swap the wicker basket for an old fishing boat but she hadn't expressly said that they COULDN'T steal an old boat and swap it for the wicker basket either, had she?

This was the argument she tried on Captain Preen, and he seemed happy to oblige. The boat was on a trailer on wheels and, between them, they managed to roll it into place. By now Preen had taken off his jacket to reveal that his smart white pilot's shirt was really collar and cuffs worn over a string vest.

Attaching the boat to the balloon wasn't an easy job, though. Jilly was sensible enough to make sure that they tied the boat to the ground before they started fixing the ropes from the balloon to it, but more than once a rope broke free and they had to grab hold of it quickly and pull it back down again.

Finally, all the ropes that had attached the balloon to the basket were now tied to the boat. They were ready. Jilly Cheeter and Teakwood Preen climbed aboard.

'Hmmm,' said Jilly. 'How are we going to release ourselves from the ropes tying us to the ground?'

'Easy,' said Preen, who looked strange with his starched shirt cuffs (with tiny gold aeroplane cufflinks) held on his wrists with elastic bands. 'I found this in the basket.' He picked up a small axe and began chopping through ropes.

Chop! Chop! Chop! Chop! Chop! – er – *Chop!*

The boat stayed firmly on the ground.

'It's too heavy!' said Jilly.

'Then we'll make it lighter!' said the captain. He began hacking off pieces of the boat with the axe and throwing them overboard on to the grass. The boat shifted and bobbed but didn't actually take off.

'I've an idea!' he said, clambering out of the boat.

Jilly Cheeter didn't get to find out what the idea was because, the moment Captain Teakwood Preen was out on the grass, the helium balloon lifted the boat – with Jilly in it – high up into the air.

As for Flabby Gomez, he was no longer lying on his back looking up at the sky. He was no longer in the water. He was sitting on top of a rock shaped like a toaster. So were the others. They had formed a circle, facing outwards so they could see the shark if it came for them again. The mayor was now holding the pizza paddle, Furl Claptrap the *Lazy Suzy* sign and Lefty Scorn still gripped the deck mop. They weren't using them as oars any more, but as clubs.

A number of times the shark had jumped out of the water to try to bite them, and a number of times they'd bopped it on the nose. Mango Claptrap would have felt happier if he'd had some kind of weapon, but there weren't enough to go round.

In Grubtown there's something called Let's Hit Lots of Things With Lots of Others Things Day where everyone gathers in Brambly Park, near the old mattresses, and has exactly one hour to hit as many things as possible with as many other things as possible — except for people, animals, plants and anything to do with Big Man Gomez (such as memorial benches, the fountain, statues or the Big Man Gomez Memorial Toilets).

There's usually a riot afterwards, so the Grubtown Police Force stay well away and there are stalls selling sticking plasters, bandages and even crutches. Doctor Fraud is always on hand to help the more seriously injured, and there are photographers from the local newspapers* who like to take 'funny photos' for the middle pages.

Mango's dad, Furl Claptrap, who is very strong (so his arms very rarely get tired), had been crowned King of Let's Hit Lots of Things With Lots of Other Things Day for six years out of seven. (One year he lost to a mysterious silver stranger from the nearby village of Werty, who later turned out to be a robot. During the

*The Grubtown Daily Herald and
The Grubtown Weekly Gerald

riot, its head fell off.) Furl used his hitting skills to great effect when the shark came. Once he thought he had hit it so hard that it might do the sensible thing and swim away and LEAVE THEM ALONE but, sadly, it came back.

'What I want to know is why the coastguard haven't rescued us by now!' said Mayor Gomez. 'If they were based in Grubtown, I'd fire the lot of them.'

'I'm sure they're looking for us,' said Lefty Scorn.

'They can't be far off,' said Furl Claptrap.

Unfortunately, both of them were wrong.

Those of you who have already read an earlier **GRuBtoWN taLe** called *The Wrong End of the Dog* may well remember the trouble Chief Grabby Hanson had with Limp coastguard's helicopter when he borrowed it. The helicopter, which they call 'the whirligig' is very old and, since then, some of the parts had been replaced with bits from old lawnmowers. It was still very good at taking off, though. Seven or eight times out of ten it would get off the ground with nothing major falling off it (unless you count Major Trowel, who often fell out of his seat and out of the copter because the chopper doesn't have doors). It's one of those helicopters with a big see-through bubble of a cockpit. It looked a bit like a giant goldfish bowl.

It looked even *more* like a goldfish bowl, now that it was filling with water. Sadly, after a spectacularly speedy and successful take-off to go to the rescue of the crew of the *Lazy Suzy*, it soon ran out of fuel and had to ditch in the sea. A later investigation reported the following findings:

1. The fuel tank of the whirligig leaked.

2. The repairs to the leaking fuel tank never seemed to stop it leaking for very long.

3. The coastguard didn't have enough money for a new fuel tank.

4. The person whose job it was to keep on repairing the leak got fed up with repairing it. He wanted

something different to repair for a change.

5. He decided to paint a little red needle on the glass on the front of the fuel gauge, pointing to 'full', so it looked as though the fuel wasn't leaking out any more.

6. But it was.

7. And a whirligig without fuel falls out of the sky.

This would have left the coastguards aboard the Limp lifeboat with a tricky decision: should they go and rescue the mayor of nearby Grubtown first and *then* the people from their own helicopter, or should they rescue their colleagues from the helicopter first and then Grubtown's mayor?

But this wasn't a decision they actually had to make.

Why not?

I'll tell you why not, and thank you for asking. (I knew I could rely on you to ask the right questions.)

When Limp coastguard's whirligig ran out of fuel – even though the little red needle on the fuel gauge was showing it to have a full tank – and the rotor blades stopped spinning and the helicopter fell into the sea, it hit the Limp lifeboat, the *Unsinkable Kitty Skittle* . . .

. . . causing her to sink.

When they'd included the word 'unsinkable' in her name, they hadn't considered the possibility of the boat being hit from above by a helicopter.

Fortunately, none of the crew in the whirligig or the lifeboat was seriously injured. Unfortunately,

they were in the sea
waving their arms
about with no
one nearby to
rescue them,
because they
were supposed
to be the rescuers.

And there were
Flabby Gomez, Mango Claptrap, Furl Claptrap
and Lefty Scorn all sitting on a rock shaped
like a toaster thinking that help was at hand.
It'd be funny, if the shark hadn't gone off to find
its fellow sharks, and hadn't brought them back
with him.

Soon the rock was being circled by a whole
gang of them.

97

Chapter Ten
Now what?

Jilly wasn't having any problems floating upwards. The problem was flying in the right direction . . . out to sea, for example. She had no idea how you were supposed to do that in a helium balloon. Free-Kick the rat had no idea either, of course, but – funnily enough – it was he who solved the problem for her.

He'd been running up and down the ropes and generally making encouraging ratty noises when they'd been preparing for lift-off. (Free-Kick was a very smart rat before he met Emily Blotch and is an even smarter one today.) Now he was on board with Jilly, watching the captain shouting and waving down below, he decided to run up one of the ropes on to the balloon itself.

He had just reached the second '**S**' of the **STOP BEING QUITE SO FAT** logo when he accidentally punctured the balloon with his teeth or his claws or both.

Before anyone knew what was happening – him on the balloon, Jilly in the boat, Preen on the ground or Sloop Cheeter in the control tower – there was a noise like one of the cows at *Wretching's Dairy* makes when she's eaten too much grass and has an ENORMOUS AMOUNT OF WIND escape from her bottom,

and the helium balloon started shooting
around the sky like a party balloon that
has broken free before its end is properly
tied in a knot.

As the helium shot out of the balloon
– with the boat still attached to it – it
swooped and dooped and looped-the-
loop and *WHOOOSHED* at incredibly
high speed, whisking Jilly Cheeter and
Free-Kick out to sea.

★ ★ ★

'Ssh!' said Mango. 'I can hear something.'

'Your father hitting sharks with one of those giant wooden paddles they usually use at Upstairs at Ample Saki's to get pizzas in and out of their special clay pizza oven?' asked Lefty Scorn. (They'd dropped the mop, which had floated off, and one of the sharks had already eaten the *Lazy Suzy* sign.)

'Apart from that!' said Mango. 'Ssh!'

They all ssh-ed, except for his dad who was still trying to stop the sharks from leaping up and snatching them off the toaster-shaped rock.

'I can hear it too!' said Flabby Gomez. 'It sounds like an enormous –'

FFFFFFFFFZZZZZZZ!

The balloon seemed to appear out of nowhere, zigzagging above them in the clear blue sky before, just as suddenly, stopping.

Silence.

The last piece of gas had escaped from the balloon.

It was flat.

It was empty.

There was nothing to hold up the clinker-built fishing boat.

It fell from the sky, with an incredible SMACK!

Actually, it was more of a:

SMACK!

and even that doesn't do it justice. It was *such* a loud SMACK that all the sharks instantly got headaches and, for just a moment, went fuzzy around the edges (like when someone gets an electric shock in a cartoon). Dazed, they drifted from the toaster-shaped rock.

Fortunately for all involved, the boat didn't land on top of Mango and the others. Imagine how embarrassing *that* would have been.

Equally fortunately, thanks to the skill of the original boat builder and Luminous Shard who had been repairing it in his spare time at the airport – when not working on aeroplane engines – the boat didn't break up and sink.

Then there was the fortunate fact that, thanks to a mixture of luck, holding on for dear-life and having had the sense to pull on a life-saver ring, Jilly Cheeter only had the wind knocked out of her when the boat hit the water. She felt like her feet were in her mouth and she wasn't sure where her head was but apart from that – and feeling very puzzled – she was fine.

What was puzzling Jilly was that it was raining money. There were banknotes fluttering everywhere and the surface of the sea round her was littered with them. It was like being in the middle of a giant, soggy wedding with confetti everywhere.

She came to her senses when she heard a cheer, followed by an amazed Mango Claptrap saying, 'Jilly?'

'What kept you?' demanded Flabby Gomez, who would have sounded more annoyed if he wasn't happily plucking FREE MONEY out of the sky. 'Now, will somebody please get us out of here?'

Free-Kick ran round the life-saver ring Jilly Cheeter was wearing around her waist. He looked up at Jilly and, she swore to me later, gave her the thumbs-up.

That night, there was a happy sight from the beach near **THE RUSTY DOLPHIN CAFE**: Chief Grabby Hanson steering Barton Wretching's *Bovine Beauty* to the jetty with Officer Mustard Tripwire at his side, and a fishing boat in tow. The boat contained a jubilant Jilly Cheeter and the rescued crew of the *Lazy Suzy* AND a bunch of highly embarrassed lifeboat and whirligig crew. Grubtown's mascot, Jip the pelican, stood proudly on the boat's prow. The mayor appeared to be clutching large amounts of *cash*.

People lined the shore to give them a heroes' welcome. News of Jilly Cheeter's bravery had spread far and wide. Within a matter of days, the Grumbly girls would have written a whole song about it and sung it outside her house at six o'clock in the morning. However, at this time, they were amongst just a handful of Grubtowners blissfully unaware of what was happening. (The girls were trapped in a lift in an underground car park over in Limp, and no one was ever able to prove whether it was an accident or not.)

Teakwood Preen (now dressed as an admiral in the navy) was on the jetty to greet them. With the only other plane grounded, Sloop Cheeter had closed FLAB-GO INTERNATIONAL for the night and was alongside him. He was relieved that his daughter was fine and Harvey was recovering at Barty Growbag's overnight after successful surgery, so what was the point of getting in a flap over 'what ifs'?

Mrs Awning was there too but, when the crowd pressed forward, she lost her footing and almost fell off the jetty where she was standing and into the sea. She grabbed the nearest

thing to steady herself, which turned out to be Binkey's beak. The pelican bit her.

Condo Blotch was there on the jetty too, along with her daughter Emily, proud of the part her **STOP BEING QUITE SO FAT** balloon had played in the rescue.

A few days later, the Condo family had even *more* reason to be proud. The mayor held a special award ceremony where he handed out a number of medals. The first medal Flabby Gomez awarded was to himself, for keeping the

other three afloat.

The second he awarded to Mango Claptrap for keeping everyone organised in the water, and for not being (1) the person who'd caused the yacht to sink in the first place (in other words Furl Claptrap) nor (2) the idiot who'd invited him out on such a dangerous trip (in other words Lefty Scorn). Jilly stomped and wolf-whistled, just happy that her best friend was alive.

The third medal went to Jilly Cheeter for

being the bravest of them all, landing in a boat from the sky – stunning the sharks in the process – and managing to get it over to the toaster-shaped rock so they could all climb aboard. Mango Claptrap beamed such a big smile at her that he looked like he'd had extra teeth added especially for the occasion.

But there was a fourth medal. This was awarded to the mayor's former shed mate – like a flatmate, but in a shed – Free-Kick, for his part in the rescue. Emily Blotch clapped the hardest as she watched Free-Kick bound across the jetty to receive it. I expect Free-Kick's mate Lulu would have clapped too, but she was quite happy just sitting on Emily's lap right at the front.

For weeks, the talk in Grubtown was about little other than the *Lazy Suzy* sinking, Limp coastguard's helicopter crashing into the lifeboat, and it raining money.

Oh yes, the money.

That must have been left over from Big Man Gomez's smuggling days, hidden away in the very heart of an old land-locked boat where no one would find it, until Luminous Shard had come across the old boat, overgrown with vines, on its side in a scrubby patch of trees around the back of the hangar. And until that boat fell from the sky and hit the sea.

The Grubtown Daily Herald summed up the whole adventure in one neat headline, which I'm sure they won't mind I've 'borrowed' for the title of this book. So let me end with it, even though there are many more **GRuBtoWN taLes** to tell:

SPLASH, CRASH AND LOADS OF CASH.

THE END

More words from Beardy Ardagh

S ome people seem to think that I really am
grumpy – even when I'm not – and some
people seem to think that I'm just pretending
to be grumpy – even when I'm not – in the
hope that it puts you off writing to me about
GRuBtoWN taLes. Grumpy or not, if you DO
write, I suggest you address the envelope:

Beardy Ardagh,
c/o Faber & Faber,
Bloomsbury House
74-77 Great Russell Street
London
WC1B 3DA

and write **GRuBtoWN taLes** in the bottom left-hand corner.

If you're hoping for a reply, <u>**DON'T FORGET TO INCLUDE A STAMPED SELF-ADDRESSED ENVELOPE**</u>. (I'm not going to buy any stamps myself. I'd rather spend my money on important things such as bread and water, to STAY ALIVE.) Not that I can promise you'll get a reply, of course. I may peel off the stamps and use them to wallpaper a wall.

You can also check out my website at www.philipardagh.com, unless it's broken, which it probably will be.

(Just some of) the folk who pop up in GRuBtoWN taLes

Jilly Cheeter girl and one-time duck-gatherer

Mango Claptrap a short boy in short trousers, whatever the weather

Manual Org a smooth-skinned fellow

Flabby Gomez Mayor of Grubtown

Hacking-Cough Gomez the mayor's brother

Big Man Gomez the mayor's dead dad

Pritt Gomez the mayor's wife

Tundra Gomez the mayor's son and heir

Kumquat 'Grabby' Hanson the chief of police

Chumbly Grumbly father to the Grumbly girls (poor man)

The Grumbly girls the seven Grumbly daughters

Formal Dripping official village idiot for the nearby village of Werty

Derek, Bunty, Shaun, Mantle, Fastbuck & Garrideb Fox the duck-hating Fox family of humans (not foxes)

Rambo Sanskrit council job-giver-outer

Sonia Pipkin local builder

The troll inhabitant of Beardy Ardagh's airing cupboard

Mrs Awning town accident-waiting-to-happen, first name unknown

Carlo Monte the riverboat gambler

Minty Glibb owner of Minty's Cake Shop

Mickey 'Steamroller' Johnson doughnut-loving steamroller driver

Leggy Prune the future Mrs Johnson

Mrs Johnson the former Leggy Prune

Paul Lutz, one-time security guard, now has senior position in Condo Blotch's NOT QUITE SO FAT business empire

Hepcat Lutz postman and amateur bug collector (of amateur bugs)

Mustard Tripwire an officer of the law and Gelatine's nephew

Galaxy Tripwire a train driver and former beauty queen

Relish Tripwire a tropical fish salesperson

Informative Boothe a very knowledgeable chap

Hobo Browne a gentleman of the road/smelly tramp

Farflung Heaps self-appointed leader of an angry mob

Garlic Hamper the lighthouse keeper

Shoona Loose the world-famous singer who does a lot for animal charities

Constable Gelatine a police sergeant

Tawdry Hipbone movie star

Snooks Miss Hipbone's pampered pooch

Luminous Shard bald heckler and mechanic

Lefty Scorn proprietor of Scorn's Laundrette & Jeweller's

Acrid Scorn an irresponsible dumper of hazardous waste

Jip the town pelican (official mascot)

Marley Gripe a painter of signs

Doctor Fraud a pretend doctor (but he's cheap)

Sloop Cheeter Jilly's dad

Harvey the Cheeter family dog

Furl Claptrap Mango's dad

Carport Claptrap Mango's mum

Vestige Claptrap Mango's brother

Claws their cat

Partial Coggs Grubtown's resident artist

Slackjaw Gumshoe paint & hardware store owner

Purple Outing very rich owner of Purple Outing's Music Shack

Hind-Leg Outing amongst other things, mother of Purple's vast number of children

Sandy Outing one of the many Outing children

Wide Brim Petty-Mandrake a regular complainer

Hetty Glue-Pen cinema manager and projectionist

Condo Blotch former cleaner now head of her very own keep-fit and health-food empire

Emily Blotch Condo's daughter

Captain Teakwood Preen man of mystery

119

Free-Kick leader of the escaped lab rats

Lulu Free-Kick's mate for life

Hardfast Tendril Grubtown's chief forester

Paltry Feedback a printer and cake decorator

Careworn Wormwood nine-day king of Grubtown

Glowering Silt general manager of Fettle's hotel

Avid Folklore manager of Fettle's hotel

Chevvy Offal owner of Offal's Sunbeds

Premix Stipend victim of one of Offal's sunbeds

Pageant Conquest food-maker (and Grabby
Hanson's sister)

Humdrum Topaz security guard and part-time
singer

Mossy Edging a very fair judge who doesn't take
bribes that often

Hybrid Byword the (now dead) TV chef

Limbo Goulash an office worker

Clam Wretching founder of Wretching's Dairy

Barton Wretching her son and current owner of
the dairy

Barty Growbag the best vet in Grubtown. (The
ONLY vet in Grubtown.)

Beardy Ardagh honoured citizen of Grubtown and
the teller of these tales

The delightful Beardy Ardagh tells of other GRuBtoWN taLes

There are important things in life and there are *un*important things. One of the most important things – if not THE most important thing – is ME. Something else which is important is that you read ALL of my GRuBtoWN taLes. Just to make absolutely sure that you've read each and every one of those published so far, I've taken the time and trouble to tell you a bit about them (except for this one), over the next few pages. Because I've taken the effort to write this, the least you can do is make the effort to read it.

RIGHT NOW.

GRuBtoWN taLes
Book One

StinkiNg Rich aNd Just PlaiN StiNky

Grubtown is full of oddballs — from the singing Grumbly girls to a family of duck-haters, and an outsized mayor who's knitting a new house — but Manual Org is too repulsive even for them. Getting him to leave town is top priority, until the discovery of a humongous diamond changes everything.

WinneR of the Roald Dahl FunNy Prize

GRuBtoWN taLes
Book Two

The YeaR That It RaiNed Cows

A startled cow falling out of nowhere onto Limbo Goulash while he's riding Marley Gripe's bicycle marks the start of a chain of events strange even by Grubtown's standards. Soon damaged property includes **PURPLE OUTING'S MUSIC SHACK** and Minty Glibb's attempt at the world's largest (strawberry) jelly-trifle. With Mayor Flabby Gomez throwing a wobbly, all chief of police, Grabby Hanson, can do is have the cow-fearing townsfolk watch the skies. Underground, meanwhile, there lies another big surprise.

GRuBtoWN taLes
Book Three

The FaR FroM GReat Escape

When the local lighthouse is plunged into darkness and a ship runs aground – flattening **THE RUSTY DOLPHIN** – it's hard to imagine things can get much worse in Grubtown. But then there's a jailbreak and the Police Department (all three of them) needs all the help it can get from the (often bonkers) townsfolk. No wonder more trouble is waiting just around the corner.

GRuBtoWN taLes
Book Four

The WRoNg ENd of the Dog

When famous film star Tawdry Hipbone visits Grubtown for the world premiere of her latest movie, *For the Love of Ducks II*, Mayor Flabby Gomez couldn't be more excited but, as usual, nothing goes to plan. Miss Hipbone's dog, Snooks, is snatched by a low-flying pelican, and it's a race against time to find him, in a rescue attempt involving Grubtown's usual ragbag of bungling buffoons.

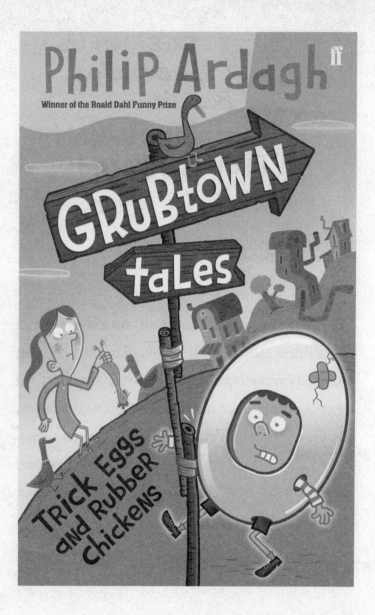

Philip Ardagh

ff

Winner of the Roald Dahl Funny Prize

GRuBtoWN

taLes

Trick Eggs
and RubbeR
chickens

GRuBtoWN taLes
Book Five

Trick Eggs and Rubber Chickens

or

Making a Splash

Everything in Grubtown should be very lovely. Mayor Flabby Gomez has finally finished knitting his new house, and the brand new Grubtown Aquarium and Carwash is about to open its leaky doors . . . but with the duck-hating Fox family out for revenge and some seriously dodgy dealings, things are about to get about as crazy as the townsfolk!

Grubtown Tourist Board

Visit www.visitgrubtown.com

Create your own Grubtown name, try your
hand at reporting for The Grubtown Daily
Herald and see what other silliness the tourist
board has in store for you.

Watch out for the ducks!